THIS BLOOMSBURY BOOK

BELONGS TO

4

....

For Joss, Mia, Matty, Molly and Aran – BE
For Christine – AF

Bloomsbury Publishing, London, Berlin and New York

First published in Great Britain in 2002 by Bloomsbury Publishing Plc,
36 Soho Square, London, W1D 3QY

This paperback edition first published in July 2003

Text copyright © Becky Edwards 2002
Illustrations copyright © Anthony Flintoft 2002

A CIP catalogue record of this book is available from the British Library

ISBN 978 0 7475 6114 9

Printed in China by South China Printing Co., Dongguan City, Guangdong

5 7 9 10 8 6

All papers used by Bloomsbury Publishing are natural, recyclable products made
from wood grown in well-managed forests. The manufacturing processes conform to
the environmental regulations of the country of origin

www.bloomsbury.com

My First Day At Nursery

Becky Edwards
and Anthony Flintoft

BLOOMSBURY

LONDON BERLIN NEW YORK

Today is a very important day for me.
Today is my first day at nursery.

My mum holds my hand until we get to the door of the nursery and then she says goodbye and a friendly lady holds my hand and takes me into a great big room.

But I don't want to be in a great big room.

I want my mum.

There are lots of toys to play with at nursery.
There is even a playhouse with a blue tea set
and a toy cooker.

There are some blue
pans for cooking
and wooden
spoons for stirring.

But I don't want a playhouse or a tea set
or a toy cooker.

I want my . . .

You can do paintings at nursery.

There are lots of different colours and you can use sponges to paint different shapes.

There is even one in the shape of a star.

But I don't want to do painting or make different shapes.

I want . . .

You can do amazing
sticking at nursery.

You can use shiny paper

or soft cotton wool

or bits of string.

There's even some sparkly glue,

but you have to be very careful not to get it
on your fingers.

But I don't want to do sticking or be careful

I . . .

We have a drink and biscuit at nursery

and then we sing some songs and dance to music.

There are even musical
instruments to play.
I play the drums
and the jingles.

I like the jingles best because they have lots of
shiny bells that you can shake.

There are lots of children to play with at nursery.

We do running

and
jumping

and chase each other round
and round.

It is very funny, especially when
you fall down
BUMP!
and then . . .

Mum arrives to take me home.

But I don't want to go home . . .

I want to play in the playhouse
and do painting

and sticking

and play the jingles

and run around with my new friends.

I want to stay at nursery.

Tomorrow is an important day for me.
Tomorrow is my second day at nursery.

And I can't wait!